CINDERELLA

AND OTHER GIRLS WHO LOST THEIR SLIPPERS

Amelia Carruthers

ORIGINS OF FAIRY TALES
FROM AROUND THE WORLD

Contents

An Introduction to

the Fairy Tale

Fairy Tales are told in almost every society, all over the globe. They have the ability to inspire generations of young and old alike, yet fail to fit neatly into any one mode of storytelling. Today, most people know these narratives through literary works or even film versions, but this is a far cry from the genre's early development. Most of the stories began, and are still propagated through oral traditions, which are still very much alive in certain cultures. Especially in rural, poorer regions, the telling of tales – from village to village, or from elder to younger, preserves culture and custom, whilst still enabling the teller to vary, embellish or adapt the tale as they see fit.

To provide a brief attempt at definition, a fairy tale is a type of short story that typically features 'fantasy' characters, such as dwarves, elves, fairies, giants, gnomes, goblins, mermaids, trolls or witches, and usually magic or enchantments to boot! Fairy tales may be distinguished from other folk narratives such as legends (which generally involve belief in the veracity of the events described) and explicitly moral tales, including fables or those of a religious nature. In cultures where demons and witches are perceived as real, fairy tales may merge into legends, where the narrative is perceived both by teller and hearers as being grounded in historical truth. However unlike legends and epics, they usually do not contain more than superficial references to religion and actual places, people, and events; they take place 'once upon a time' rather than in reality.

The history of the fairy tale is particularly difficult to trace, as most often, it is only the literary forms that are available to the scholar. Still, written evidence indicates that fairy tales have existed for thousands of years, although not perhaps recognized as a genre. Many of today's fairy narratives have evolved from centuries-old stories that have appeared, with variations, in multiple cultures around the world. Two theories of origins have attempted to explain the common elements in fairy tales across continents. One is that a single point of origin generated any given tale, which then spread over the centuries. The other is that such fairy tales stem from common human experience and therefore can appear separately in many different origins. Debates still rage over which interpretation is correct, but as ever, it is likely that a combination of both aspects are involved in the advancements of these folkloric chronicles.

Some folklorists prefer to use the German term *Märchen* or 'wonder tale' to refer to the genre over *fairy tale,* a practice given weight by the definition of Thompson in his 1977 edition of *The Folktale.* He described it as 'a tale of some length involving a succession of motifs or episodes. It moves in an unreal world without definite locality or definite creatures and is filled with the marvellous. In this never-never land, humble heroes kill adversaries, succeed to kingdoms and marry princesses.' The genre was first marked out by writers of the Renaissance, such as Giovanni Francesco Straparola and Giambattista Basile, and stabilized through the works of later collectors such as Charles Perrault and the Brothers Grimm. The oral tradition of the fairy tale came long before the written page however.

Tales were told or enacted dramatically, rather than written down, and handed from generation to generation. Because of this, many fairy tales appear in written literature throughout different cultures, as in *The Golden Ass,* which includes *Cupid and Psyche* (Roman, 100–200 CE), or the *Panchatantra* (India, 3rd century CE). However it is still unknown to what extent these reflect the actual folk tales even of their own time. The 'fairy tale' as a genre became popular among the French nobility of the seventeenth century, and among the tales told were the *Contes* of Charles Perrault (1697), who fixed the forms of 'Sleeping Beauty' and 'Cinderella.' Perrault largely laid the foundations for this new literary variety, with some of the best of his works including 'Puss in Boots', 'Little Red Riding Hood' and 'Bluebeard'.

The first collectors to attempt to preserve not only the plot and characters of the tale, but also the style in which they were told were the Brothers Grimm, who assembled German fairy tales. The Brothers Grimm rejected several tales for their anthology, though told by Germans, because the tales derived from Perrault and they concluded that the stories were thereby *French* and not *German* tales. An oral version of 'Bluebeard' was thus rejected, and the tale of 'Little Briar Rose', clearly related to Perrault's 'The Sleeping Beauty' was included only because Jacob Grimm convinced his brother that the figure of *Brynhildr*, from much earlier Norse mythology, proved that the sleeping princess was authentically German. The Grimm Brothers remain some of the best-known story-tellers of folk tales though, popularising 'Hansel and Gretel', 'Rapunzel', 'Rumplestiltskin' and 'Snow White.'

The work of the Brothers Grimm influenced other collectors, both inspiring them to collect tales and leading them to similarly believe, in a spirit of romantic nationalism, that the fairy tales of a country were particularly representative of it (unfortunately generally ignoring any cross-cultural references). Among those influenced were the Norwegian Peter Christen Asbjørnsen (*Norske Folkeeventyr*, 1842-3), the Russian Alexander Afanasyev (*Narodnye Russkie Skazki,* 1855-63) and the Englishman, Joseph Jacobs (*English Fairy Tales,* 1890). Simultaneously to such developments, writers such as Hans Christian Andersen and George MacDonald continued the tradition of penning original literary fairy tales. Andersen's work sometimes drew on old folktales, but more often deployed fairytale motifs and plots in new stories; for instance in 'The Little Mermaid', 'The Ugly Duckling' and 'The Emperor's New Clothes.'

Fairy tales are still written in the present day, attesting to their enormous popularity and cultural longevity. Aside from their long and diverse literary history, these stories have also been stunningly illustrated by some of the world's best artists – as the reader will be able to see in the following pages. The Golden Age of Illustration (a period customarily defined as lasting from the latter quarter of the nineteenth century until just after the First World War) produced some of the finest examples of this craft, and the masters of the trade are all collected in this volume, alongside the original, inspiring tales. These images form their own story, evolving in conjunction with the literary development of the tales. Consequently, the illustrations are presented in their own narrative sequence, for the reader to appreciate *in and of themselves*. An introduction to the 'Golden Age' can also be found at the end of this book.

The History of Cinderella

Cinderella is one of the best known stories of all time. It has appeared across many different eras, in many different cultures, and according to varying estimations, there could be anything between 350 and 1500 different versions of the tale. The very basics of the narrative revolve around a kind and just young woman (the Cinderella character), who suffers some form of unjust oppression – usually at the hands of her step-family. The supernatural element comes in the form of a guardian (referred to as the 'Fairy Godmother' in the European tradition), who enables Cinderella to be recognized for her true worth. But aside from this rough narrative framework, story-tellers around the world have varied the literary details with considerable panache.

The earliest recorded version of the Cinderella story comes from Egypt. The oral tale of Rhodopis and Her Little Gilded Sandals depicts a Greek slave girl who eventually marries the king of Egypt. It was first recorded by a Greek geographer (Strabo) in the first century BCE. Aside from another retelling by the Roman historian Claudius Aelianus in Varia Historia, few versions appeared until Tuan Ch'eng-shih penned a variant of the tale in ninth century China. From the way in which it was written, it is thought that Chinese readers were already familiar with the chain of events. This is in itself is nothing surprising, as most folk and fairy tales emerged in the spoken tradition, but what is thoroughly intriguing, is the spread of this idiomatic tale. How did it travel from first century Greece, to ninth century China (with little evidence of its progress in-between) – and then sink into little known obscurity before appearing in seventeenth century France?

Folklorists have indeed long studied versions of this tale across cultures. In 1893, Marian Roalfe Cox, commissioned by the Folklore Society of Britain, produced *Cinderella: Three Hundred and Forty-Five Variants of Cinderella,*

Catskin and, Cap o'Rushes, Abstracted and Tabulated with a Discussion of Medieval Analogues and Notes. A lot of attention, perhaps unsurprisingly, has been paid to Cinderella's lost slipper; a mark of feminine beauty and daintiness. The slipper is of red satin in Madame d'Aulnoy's *Finette Cendron* (1697) and of plain satin in Joseph Jacob's *Rashin-Coatie* (1894). The test of fitting the owner recurs in *Peau d'Ane* (another Perrault tale), where a ring, not a slipper is the object, and the same is the case in *The Wonderful Birch* (a Finnish/Russian variant). What is especially interesting about these stories though, is not the archetypal 'princess' moments, but how older, generally much more barbaric variations have been bowdlerized by subsequent authors.

In many older examples of this story (as we have already seen), the fairy godmother role is played by a friendly beast or object. Early societies (especially Indian tribes) transformed their beast-ancestors (totems) into the figures of human ancestors with similar names. Correspondingly, as this process happened over time, the roles filled by beasts in the early European *Märchen* came to be assigned to men and women in later versions of the tales. In *The Wonderful Birch*, the place of the friendly beast is taken by the ghost of the protagonist's mother (who had been turned into a sheep, murdered and eaten). In a modern Greek version, the mother is eaten by her daughters except the youngest (the Cinderella character), who refuses the hideous meal. The dead woman magically aids the youngest, and the rest of the narrative follows as usual. In the Scottish variant of *Rashin-Coatie,* the mother dies – but leaves her daughter a red calf which aids her, until it is slain by a cruel stepmother. At this point, similarly to the Russian story, the daughter buries her bones under a stone where she is thereafter granted wishes. The idea of a mother's love surviving her death inspires this legend, and despite the many savage details, the stories produce a touching effect.

Perhaps the second most prominent version (after Perrault's) is the Brothers Grimm's *Aschenputtel* (1812). The supernatural 'help' in this account also comes from a wishing tree that grows on her mother's grave. Unlike other variants though, Aschenputtel's relationship with her father is ambiguous. Perrault's version states that the absent father is dominated by his second wife, explaining why he does not prevent the abuse of his daughter. However, the father in the Grimm's tale plays an active role in several scenes, and it is not explained why he tolerates the mistreatment of his child. In such folktales there is often a favoritism (shown by the author, if not the parents) for the youngest child, and the custom which allots this child a place by the hearth or in the cinders ('cencere', 'cendres', 'asche'). This notion declares itself in the various names of Cinderella; *Aschenputtel, Ventafochs, Pepelluga, Cernushka,* all signifying blackness – chiefly from contact with the coals.

Perrault understood the story as having two morals, firstly that 'beauty is a treasure, but graciousness is priceless' and secondly that: 'Without doubt it is a great advantage to have intelligence, courage, good breeding, and common sense. These, and similar talents come only from heaven, and it is good to have them. However, even these may fail to bring you success, without the blessing of a godfather or a godmother.' Here, even in this later 'tamed' version, the timeless virtue of loyalty to one's kin (and love in return) is seen as the ultimate graciousness. As a testament to this storie's ability to inspire and entertain generations of readers, the *Cinderella* tale continues to influence popular culture internationally, lending plot elements, allusions, and tropes to a wide variety of artistic mediums. It has been translated into fifty languages, and very excitingly, is continuing to evolve in the present day. We hope the reader enjoys this collection of some of its best re-tellings.

Rhodopis and Her Little Gilded Sandals

(An Egyptian Tale)

This tale, a narrative of Egyptian origin, is the earliest known variant of the 'Cinderella Story.' It was first recorded by a Greek geographer, Strabo (C. 64 BCE - 24 CE), in his *Geographica* (Book XVII). The chronicle depicts a Greek slave girl, Rhodopis (translating as 'Rosey-Eyes'), who lived in the colony of Naucratis in Ancient Egypt. Strabo recounts how an eagle snatched the young girl's sandals while she was bathing, and dropped them into the King's lap. The king, entranced, sent his men to search for the woman to whom the shoes belonged. Once she was found, Rhodopis was brought to the King, they married – and lived happily ever after.

Herodotus (c. 484 - 425 BCE), some five centuries before Strabo, supplied information about the real-life Rhodopis in his *Histories*. He wrote that Rhodopis came from Thrace, and was the slave of Iadmon of Samos, and a fellow-slave of the story-teller Aesop. She was taken to Egypt in the time of Pharaoh Amasis, and freed there by the brother of Sappho the lyric poet. Another synopsis is given by the Roman author Aelian (c. 175 - 235), showing that the Cinderella theme remained popular throughout antiquity.

$$\longrightarrow$$

Her Mother knew so many stories that she could tell a new one every night almost.
Cinderella - Retold by C. S. Evans, 1909.
Illustrated by Arthur Rackham

- Whilst visiting the Egyptian pyramids, Strabo recounted the tale of the 'Tomb of the Courtesan':

... Having been built by her lovers — the courtesan whom Sapphothe Melic poetess calls Doricha, the beloved of Sappho's brother Charaxus, who was engaged in transporting Lesbian wine to Naucratis for sale, but others give her the name Rhodopis.

They tell the fabulous story that, when she was bathing, an eagle snatched one of her sandals from her maid and carried it to Memphis; and while the king was administering justice in the open air, the eagle, when it arrived above his head, flung the sandal into his lap; and the king, stirred both by the beautiful shape of the sandal and by the strangeness of the occurrence, sent men in all directions into the country in quest of the woman who wore the sandal; and when she was found in the city of Naucratis, she was brought up to Memphis, became the wife of the king, and when she died was honoured with the above-mentioned tomb.

The haughtiest, proudest woman that had ever been seen.
Old Time Stories Told by Master Charles Perrault, 1921.
Illustrated by W. Heath Robinson

CENERENTOLA

(An Italian Tale)

Cenerentola is an Italian version of the *Cinderella* story, written by *Giambattista Basile* (1566-1632). It was first published in his collection of *Neapolitan* fairy tales titled *Lo Cunto de li Cunti Overo lo Ttrattenemiento de Peccerille* (translating as 'The Tale of Tales, or Entertainment for Little Ones'), posthumously published in two volumes in 1634 and 1636.

Although neglected for some time, the work received a great deal of attention after the Brothers Grimm praised it highly as the first *national* collection of fairy tales. Many of the fairy tales that Basile collected are the oldest known variants in existence, including this - the oldest *full-length* version of the Cinderella story to be published. Unlike most other accounts, in this narrative the name of the girl is revealed as *Zezolla*, before she is given the new name of 'Cenerentola.'

>———→

In the sea of Malice Envy frequently gets out of her depth; and whilst she is expecting to see another drowned, she is either drowned herself, or is dashed against a rock, as happened to some envious girls, about whom I will tell you a story.

There once lived a prince, who was a widower, but who had a daughter, so dear to him that he saw with no other eyes than hers; and he kept a governess for her, who taught her chain-work, and knitting, and to make point-lace, and showed her such affection as no words can tell. But after a time the father married again, and took a wicked jade for his wife, who soon conceived a violent dislike to her stepdaughter; and all day long she made sour looks, wry faces and fierce eyes at her, till the poor child was beside herself with terror, and was for ever bewailing to her governess the bad treatment she received from her stepmother, saying to her, "O heavens, that you had been my mother, you who show me so much kindness and affection!" And she went on thus, sighing and singing to this tune, till at last the governess, having a wasp put in her ear and blinded by the Mazzamauriello [a wicked little imp], said to her one day, " If you will do as this foolish head of mine advises, I shall be mother to you, and you will be as dear to me as the apple of my eye."

She was going on to say more, when Zezolla (for that was the girl's name) said, "Pardon me if I stop the word upon your tongue. I know you wish me well, therefore hush! enough - only show me the way to get out of my trouble; do you write, and I will subscribe."

"Well then," answered the governess, "open your ears and listen, and you will get bread as white as the flowers. When your father goes out, ask your stepmother to give you one of the old dresses that are in the large chest in the closet, in order to save the one you have on. Then she, who would like of all things to see you go in rags and tatters, will open the chest, and say, 'Hold up the lid !' and whilst you are holding it up, and she is rummaging about inside, let it fall with a bang, so as to break her neck. When this is done, as you know well enough that your father would even coin false money to please you, do you entreat him when he is caressing you to take me to wife; for then, bless your stars - you shall be the mistress of my life."

Then Zezolla heard this, every hour seemed to her a thousand years until she had done all that her governess had advised; and as soon as the mourning for the stepmother's death was ended, she began to feel her father's pulse, and to entreat him to marry the governess. At first the prince took it as a joke, but Zezolla went on shooting so long past the mark, that at length she hit it, and he gave way to her entreaties. So he took Carmosina that was the name of the governess) to wife, and gave a great feast at the wedding.

They called the other daughter Cinderella.
The Cinderella Picture Book, 1875.
Illustrated by Walter Crane

She was made to live in a dark, stone-flagged kitchen with
nothing but rats, mice, and cockroaches for company.
Told Again - Old Tales Told Again, 1927.
Illustrated by A. H. Watson

Now whilst the young folks were dancing, and Zezolla was standing at a window of her house, a dove came flying and perched upon a wall, and said to her, "Whenever you desire anything, send the request to the Dove of the Fairies in the island of Sardinia, and you will instantly have what you wish."

For five or six days the new stepmother overwhelmed Zezolla with caresses, seating her at the best place at table, giving her the choicest morsels to eat, and clothing her in the richest apparel. But ere long forgetting entirely the good service she had received, (woe to him who has a bad master!) she began to bring forward six daughters of her own, whom she had until then kept concealed; and she praised them so much, and talked her husband over in such a manner, that at last the stepdaughters engrossed all his favor, and the thought of his own child went entirely from his heart: in short, it fared so ill with the poor girl, bad today and worse tomorrow, that she was at last brought down from the royal chamber to the kitchen, from the canopy of state to the hearth, from splendid apparel of silks and gold to dishclouts, from the scepter to the spit. And not only was her condition changed, but even her name; for instead of Zezolla, she was now called Cenerentola.

It happened that the prince had occasion to go to Sardinia upon affairs of state; and calling the six stepdaughters - Imperia, Calamita, Fiorella, Diamante, Colombina, Pascarella - he asked them one by one what they would like him to bring them on his return. Then one wished for splendid dresses, another to have head ornaments, another rouge for the face, another toys and trinkets; in short, one wished for this thing and another for that. At last the prince said to his own daughter, as if in mockery, "And what would you have, child ?"— "Nothing, father," she-replied, "but that you commend me to the Dove of the Fairies, and bid her send me something; and if you forget my request, may you be unable to stir either backwards or forwards: so remember what I tell you, for it will fare with you accordingly."

Cinderella.

Tales of Passed Times, 1900.

Illustrated by Charles Robinson

Then the prince went his way, and transacted his affairs in Sardinia, and procured all the things which his stepdaughters had asked for; but poor Zezolla went quite out of his thoughts. And embarking on board a ship, he set sail to return; but the ship could not get out of the harbor; there it stuck fast, just as if held back by a sea-lamprey. The captain of the ship, who was almost in despair and fairly tired out, laid himself down to sleep; and in his dream he saw a fairy, who said to him, "Know you the reason why you cannot work the ship out of port ? it is because the prince who is on board with you has broken his promise to his daughter, remembering every one except his own blood."

Then the captain awoke, and told his dream to the prince, who, in shame and confusion at the breach of his promise, went to the Grotto of the Fairies, and commending his daughter to them, asked them to send her something. And behold there stepped forth from the grotto a beautiful maiden, who told him that she thanked his daughter for her kind remembrance, and bade him tell her to be merry and of good heart, out of love to her. And thereupon she gave him a date-tree, a hoe and a little bucket all of gold, and a silken napkin; adding, that the one was to hoe with and the other to water the plant.

The prince, marveling at this present, took leave of the fairy and returned to his own country. And when he had given the stepdaughters all the things they had desired, he at last gave his own daughter the gift which the fairy had sent her. Then Zezolla, out of her wits with joy, took the date-tree and planted it in a pretty flowerpot, hoed the earth around it, watered it, and wiped its leaves morning and evening with the silken napkin; so that in a few days it had grown as tall as a woman, and out of it came a fairy, who said to Zezolla, "What do you wish for?" And Zezolla replied, that she wished sometimes to leave the house without her sisters' knowledge. The fairy answered, "Whenever you desire this, come to the flowerpot and say,

'My little Date-tree, my golden tree,
With a golden hoe I have hoed thee,
With a golden can I have water'd thee,
With a silken cloth I have wiped thee dry,
Now strip thee, and dress me speedily!'

And when you wish to undress, change the last verse, and say, "Strip me, and dress thee."

When the time for the feast was come, and the stepmother's daughters appeared, dressed out so fine, all ribbands and flowers, and slippers and shoes, sweet smells and bells, and roses and posies, Zezolla ran quickly to the flowerpot; and no sooner had she repeated the words which the fairy had told her, than she saw herself arrayed like a queen, seated upon a palfrey, and attended by twelve smart pages all dressed in their best. Then she went to the ball where the sisters had gone, whose mouths watered with envy of the beauty of this graceful dove.

Now as luck would have it the king himself came to that same place, who, as soon as he saw the marvelous beauty of Zezolla, stood magic-bound with amazement, and ordered a trusty servant to find out who that beautiful creature was, and where she lived. So the servant followed in her footsteps; but Zezolla, observing the trick, threw on the ground a handful of crown-pieces, which she had made the date-tree give her for this purpose. Then the servant lighted the lantern, and in his eagerness to fill his pockets with the crown-pieces he forgot to follow the palfrey. In the meantime Zezolla hastened home, and undressed herself as the fairy had told her. Soon afterwards the wicked sisters returned, and, in order to vex her and excite her envy, they told her of all kinds of beautiful things that they had seen.

They used to creep away to the chimney-corner and seat herself among the cinders.
The Sleeping Beauty and Other Fairy Tales From the Old French, 1910.
Illustrated by Edmund Dulac

Meanwhile the servant came back to the king, and told him what had happened with the crown-pieces; whereupon the king flew into a great rage, telling him that for a few paltry farthings he had sold his pleasure, and commanding him at all events to find out at the next feast who the beautiful maiden was, and where this pretty bird had its nest.

When the next feast was come, the sisters all went to it decked out smartly, leaving poor Zezolla at home on the hearth. Then Zezolla ran quickly to the date-tree, and repeated the words as before; and instantly there appeared a number of damsels, one with a looking-glass, another with a bottle of pumpkin-water, another with the curling-irons, another with a comb, another with pins, another with dresses, and another with capes and collars. And decking her out till she looked as beautiful as a sun, they placed her in a coach drawn by six horses, attended by footmen and pages in livery. And no sooner did she appear in the room where the former feast was held, than the hearts of the sisters were filled with amazement, and the breast of the king with fire.

When Zezolla went away again, the servant followed in her footsteps as before; but, in order not to be caught, she threw down a handful of pearls and jewels; and the good fellow, seeing that they were not things to lose, stayed to pick them up. So Zezolla had time to slip home and take off her fine dress as before.

Meanwhile the servant returned slowly to the king, who exclaimed when he saw him, "By the souls of my ancestors, if you don't find out who she is, I'll give you a sound thrashing, and, what's more, I'll give you as many kicks as you have hairs in that beard of thine!"

When the next feast was held, and the sisters had gone to it, Zezolla went to the date-tree, and repeating the words of the charm, in an instant she was splendidly arrayed, and seated in a coach of gold, with ever so many servants

Cinderella.
A Child's Book of Stories, 1914.
Illustrated by Jessie Willcox Smith

Ashputtel.

Grimm's Fairy Tales, 1902.

Illustrated by John Hassall

around, so that she looked just like a queen. The envy of the sisters was excited as before; and when she left the room, the king's servant kept close to the coach. But Zezolla, seeing that the man kept running at her side, cried, "Coachman, drive on!" and in a trice the coach set off at such a rattling pace, that Zezolla lost one of her slippers, the prettiest thing that ever was seen. The servant, being unable to overtake the coach, which flew like a bird, picked up the slipper, and carrying it to the king told him all that had happened. Whereupon the king taking it in his hand said, "If the basement indeed is so beautiful, what must the building be? O beauteous candlestick, where is the candle that consumes me? O tripod of the bright boiler in which life simmers! O beautiful cork, fastened to the angling-line of Love, with which he has caught my soul! Lo, I embrace you, I press you to my heart; and if I cannot reach the plant, I adore at least the roots; if I cannot possess the capital of the column, I kiss the base. You who until now were the prison of a white foot, are now the fetter of an unhappy heart."

So saying he called his secretary, and commanded the trumpeter to sound a "Too, too!" and make proclamation, that all the women of that country should come to a feast and banquet which he had taken it into his head to give. And when the appointed day was come, heyday, what a feasting and frolic was there! from whence in the world came all the pies and pasties? whence the stews and ragouts? whence the maccaroni and sweetmeats? In short there was enough to feed a whole army.

And when the women were all assembled, noble and ignoble, rich and poor, old and young, beautiful and ugly, and when all was ready, the king tried the slipper first on one and then on another of the guests, to see whom it should fit to a hair, and to be able thus to discover by the form of the slipper the maiden of whom he it exactly, he began to despair. However, having ordered silence, he said, "Come again tomorrow, and eat a bit of dinner with me; and as you love me, don't leave a single girl or woman at home, be she who she may." Then the prince said, "I have indeed another daughter at home; but she is always on the hearth, and is such a graceless simpleton that she is unworthy to sit down to eat at your table." But the king said, "Let her be the very first on the list, for so I will."

So all the guests departed, and the next day they assembled again, and with Carmosina's daughters came Zezolla. The instant the king saw her, he imagined it was she whom he longed to find; but this he kept to himself. And when the feasting was ended, came the trial of the slipper; but as soon as ever it approached Zezolla's foot, it darted of itself to the foot of that painted egg of Venus, as the iron flies to the magnet; at the sight of which the king ran to her and made a press for her with his arms, and seating her under the royal canopy he set the crown upon her head; whereupon all made their obeisance and homage to her as their queen.

When the sisters beheld this, they were full of spite and rage; and not having patience to look upon this object of their hatred, they slipped quietly away on tip toe, and went home to their mother, confessing in spite of themselves that "He is a madman who resists the stars."

It is impossible to conceive how much the good fortune of Zezolla touched the heart of every one present; but greatly as they praised the liberality of Heaven to the poor girl, they considered the punishment of Carmosina's daughters far too trifling; for there is no punishment which pride does not deserve, no misfortune that envy does not merit.

She was a hundred times more beautiful than her sisters could be.

Perrault's Fairy Tales, 1913.

Illustrated by Honor Appleton

The sisters called her up and said, "Now comb our hair brush our shoes,
and tie our sashes for us, for we are going to dance at the King's feast."

Grimm's Fairy Tales, 1911.

Illustrated by Charles Folkard

Cendrillon, ou La Petite Pantoufle de Verre

(A French Tale)

Cenrillon, ou La Petite Pantoufle de Verre **was penned by Charles Perrault (1628-1703), a French author and member of the Académie Française – a man largely responsible for laying the foundations of the fairy-tale genre.**

It was published in 1697, in *Histoires ou Contes du Temps Passé: Les Contes de ma Mère l'Oye* ('Tales and Stories of the Past with Morals: Tales of Mother Goose'). All of Perrault's works were based on pre-existing stories, but his flair for storytelling 'fixed' the narrative as we know it today. The general plot remained unchanged from its ancient Egyptian beginnings (a lowly, yet kind and just young woman, unfairly wronged – but eventually 'rescued' and wed by the King/Prince). However Perrault's tale became immensely popular due to his own unique additions; the pumpkin, the fairy-godmother and the introduction of the glass slippers.

Once upon a time there was a gentleman who married, for his second wife, the proudest and most haughty woman that ever was seen. She had two daughters of her own, who were, indeed, exactly like her in all things. The gentleman had also a young daughter, of rare goodness and sweetness of temper, which she took from her mother, who was the best creature in the world.

Any one but Cinderella would have dressed their heads awry.
The Fairy Tales of Charles Perrault, 1922.
Illustrated by Harry Clarke

The wedding was scarcely over, when the stepmother's bad temper began to show itself. She could not bear the goodness of this young girl, because it made her own daughters appear the more odious. The stepmother gave her the meanest work in the house to do; she had to scour the dishes, tables, etc., and to scrub the floors and clean out the bedrooms. The poor girl had to sleep in the garret, upon a wretched straw bed, while her sisters lay in fine rooms with inlaid floors, upon beds of the very newest fashion, and where they had looking-glasses so large that they might see themselves at their full length. The poor girl bore all patiently, and dared not complain to her father, who would have scolded her if she had done so, for his wife governed him entirely.

When she had done her work, she used to go into the chimney corner, and sit down among the cinders, hence she was called Cinderwench. The younger sister of the two, who was not so rude and uncivil as the elder, called her Cinderella. However, Cinderella, in spite of her mean apparel, was a hundred times more handsome than her sisters, though they were always richly dressed.

It happened that the King's son gave a ball, and invited to it all persons of fashion. Our young misses were also invited, for they cut a very grand figure among the people of the country-side. They were highly delighted with the invitation, and wonderfully busy in choosing the gowns, petticoats, and head-dresses which might best become them. This made Cinderella's lot still harder, for it was she who ironed her sisters' linen and plaited their ruffles. They talked all day long of nothing but how they should be dressed.

"For my part," said the elder, "I will wear my red velvet suit with French trimmings."

"And I," said the younger, "shall wear my usual skirt; but then, to make amends for that I will put on my gold-flowered mantle, and my diamond stomacher, which is far from being the most ordinary one in the world." They sent for the best hairdressers they could get to make up their hair in fashionable style, and bought patches for their cheeks. Cinderella was consulted in all these matters, for she had good taste. She advised them always for the best, and even offered her services to dress their hair, which they were very willing she should do.

As she was doing this, they said to her:—

"Cinderella, would you not be glad to go to the ball?"

"Young ladies," she said, "you only jeer at me; it is not for such as I am to go there."

"You are right," they replied; "people would laugh to see a Cinderwench at a ball."

Any one but Cinderella would have dressed their hair awry, but she was good-natured, and arranged it perfectly well. They were almost two days without eating, so much were they transported with joy. They broke above a dozen laces in trying to lace themselves tight, that they might have a fine, slender shape, and they were continually at their looking-glass.

At last the happy day came; they went to Court, and Cinderella followed them with her eyes as long as she could, and when she had lost sight of them, she fell a-crying.

Her godmother, who saw her all in tears, asked her what was the matter.

"I wish I could—I wish I could—" but she could not finish for sobbing.

Her godmother, who was a fairy, said to her, "You wish you could go to the ball; is it not so?"

*Looking in their wigs and powder more like bunched-up
fantastic monkeys than human beings.*

Told Again - Old Tales Told Again, 1927.

Illustrated by A. H. Watson

They went rustling and tinkling to the ball.
Tales From Grimm, 1936.
Illustrated by Wanda Gag

"Alas, yes," said Cinderella, sighing.

"Well," said her godmother, "be but a good girl, and I will see that you go." Then she took her into her chamber, and said to her, "Run into the garden, and bring me a pumpkin."

Cinderella went at once to gather the finest she could get, and brought it to her godmother, not being able to imagine how this pumpkin could help her to go to the ball. Her godmother scooped out all the inside of it, leaving nothing but the rind. Then she struck it with her wand, and the pumpkin was instantly turned into a fine gilded coach.

She then went to look into the mouse-trap, where she found six mice, all alive. She ordered Cinderella to lift the trap-door, when, giving each mouse, as it went out, a little tap with her wand, it was that moment turned into a fine horse, and the six mice made a fine set of six horses of a beautiful mouse-coloured, dapple gray.

Being at a loss for a coachman, Cinderella said, "I will go and see if there is not a rat in the rat-trap—we may make a coachman of him."

"You are right," replied her godmother; "go and look."

Cinderella brought the rat-trap to her, and in it there were three huge rats. The fairy chose the one which had the largest beard, and, having touched him with her wand, he was turned into a fat coachman with the finest moustache and whiskers ever seen.

After that, she said to her:—

"Go into the garden, and you will find six lizards behind the watering-pot; bring them to me."

She had no sooner done so than her godmother turned them into six footmen, who skipped up immediately behind the coach, with their liveries all trimmed with gold and silver, and they held on as if they had done nothing else their whole lives.

The fairy then said to Cinderella, "Well, you see here a carriage fit to go to the ball in; are you not pleased with it?"

"Oh, yes!" she cried; "but must I go as I am in these rags?"

Her godmother simply touched her with her wand, and, at the same moment, her clothes were turned into cloth of gold and silver, all decked with jewels. This done, she gave her a pair of the prettiest glass slippers in the whole world. Being thus attired, she got into the carriage, her godmother commanding her, above all things, not to stay till after midnight, and telling her, at the same time, that if she stayed one moment longer, the coach would be a pumpkin again, her horses mice, her coachman a rat, her footmen lizards, and her clothes would become just as they were before.

She promised her godmother she would not fail to leave the ball before midnight. She drove away, scarce able to contain herself for joy. The King's son, who was told that a great princess, whom nobody knew, was come, ran out to receive her. He gave her his hand as she alighted from the coach, and led her into the hall where the company were assembled. There was at once a profound silence; every one left off dancing, and the violins ceased to play, so attracted was every one by the singular beauties of the unknown newcomer. Nothing was then heard but a confused sound of voices saying:—

And they drove away, leaving poor Cinderella gazing sadly out of the window.
Cinderella - Retold by C. S. Evans, 1909.
Illustrated by Arthur Rackham

"Ha! how beautiful she is! Ha! how beautiful she is!"

The King himself, old as he was, could not keep his eyes off her, and he told the Queen under his breath that it was a long time since he had seen so beautiful and lovely a creature.

All the ladies were busy studying her clothes and head-dress, so that they might have theirs made next day after the same pattern, provided they could meet with such fine materials and able hands to make them.

The King's son conducted her to the seat of honor, and afterwards took her out to dance with him. She danced so very gracefully that they all admired her more and more. A fine collation was served, but the young Prince ate not a morsel, so intently was he occupied with her.

She went and sat down beside her sisters, showing them a thousand civilities, and giving them among other things part of the oranges and citrons with which the Prince had regaled her. This very much surprised them, for they had not been presented to her.

Cinderella heard the clock strike a quarter to twelve. She at once made her adieus to the company and hastened away as fast as she could.

As soon as she got home, she ran to find her godmother, and, after having thanked her, she said she much wished she might go to the ball the next day, because the King's son had asked her to do so. As she was eagerly telling her godmother all that happened at the ball, her two sisters knocked at the door; Cinderella opened it. "How long you have stayed!" said she, yawning, rubbing her eyes, and stretching herself as if she had been just awakened. She had not, however, had any desire to sleep since they went from home.

She sat sadly gazing into the fire.
Nursery Tales, 1923.
Illustrated by Paul Woodroffe

Her godmother found her in tears.
Old Time Stories Told by Master Charles Perrault, 1921.
Illustrated by W. Heath Robinson

"If you had been at the ball," said one of her sisters, "you would not have been tired with it. There came thither the finest princess, the most beautiful ever was seen with mortal eyes. She showed us a thousand civilities, and gave us oranges and citrons."

Cinderella did not show any pleasure at this. Indeed, she asked them the name of the princess; but they told her they did not know it, and that the King's son was very much concerned, and would give all the world to know who she was. At this Cinderella, smiling, replied:—

"Was she then so very beautiful? How fortunate you have been! Could I not see her? Ah! dear Miss Charlotte, do lend me your yellow suit of clothes which you wear every day."

"Ay, to be sure!" cried Miss Charlotte; "lend my clothes to such a dirty Cinderwench as thou art! I should be out of my mind to do so."

Cinderella, indeed, expected such an answer and was very glad of the refusal; for she would have been sadly troubled if her sister had lent her what she jestingly asked for. The next day the two sisters went to the ball, and so did Cinderella, but dressed more magnificently than before. The King's son was always by her side, and his pretty speeches to her never ceased. These by no means annoyed the young lady. Indeed, she quite forgot her godmother's orders to her, so that she heard the clock begin to strike twelve when she thought it could not be more than eleven. She then rose up and fled, as nimble as a deer. The Prince followed, but could not overtake her. She left behind one of her glass slippers, which the Prince took up most carefully. She got home, but quite out of breath, without her carriage, and in her old clothes, having nothing left her of all her finery but one of the little slippers, fellow to the one she had dropped. The guards at the palace gate were asked if they had not seen a princess go out, and they replied they had seen nobody go out but a young

Cendrillon.

Contes de Perrault, 1910.

Illustrated by Margaret Tarrant

girl, very meanly dressed, and who had more the air of a poor country girl than of a young lady.

When the two sisters returned from the ball, Cinderella asked them if they had had a pleasant time, and if the fine lady had been there. They told her, yes; but that she hurried away the moment it struck twelve, and with so much haste that she dropped one of her little glass slippers, the prettiest in the world, which the King's son had taken up. They said, further, that he had done nothing but look at her all the time, and that most certainly he was very much in love with the beautiful owner of the glass slipper.

What they said was true; for a few days after the King's son caused it to be proclaimed, by sound of trumpet, that he would marry her whose foot this slipper would fit exactly. They began to try it on the princesses, then on the duchesses, and then on all the ladies of the Court; but in vain. It was brought to the two sisters, who did all they possibly could to thrust a foot into the slipper, but they could not succeed. Cinderella, who saw this, and knew her slipper, said to them, laughing:—

"Let me see if it will not fit me."

Her sisters burst out a-laughing, and began to banter her. The gentleman who was sent to try the slipper looked earnestly at Cinderella, and, finding her very handsome, said it was but just that she should try, and that he had orders to let every lady try it on.

He obliged Cinderella to sit down, and, putting the slipper to her little foot, he found it went on very easily, and fitted her as if it had been made of wax. The astonishment of her two sisters was great, but it was still greater when Cinderella pulled out of her pocket the other slipper and put it on her foot.

Rustle and shake yourself, dear tree, and silver and gold throw down to me.
Grimm's Fairy Tales, 1929.
Illustrated by Elenore Abbott

Thereupon, in came her godmother, who, having touched Cinderella's clothes. with her wand, made them more magnificent than those she had worn before

And now her two sisters found her to be that beautiful lady they had seen at the ball. They threw themselves at her feet to beg pardon for all their ill treatment of her. Cinderella took them up, and, as she embraced them, said that she forgave them with all her heart, and begged them to love her always.

She was conducted to the young Prince, dressed as she was. He thought her more charming than ever, and, a few days after, married her. Cinderella, who was as good as she was beautiful, gave her two sisters a home in the palace, and that very same day married them to two great lords of the Court.

Shake, shake, hazel-tree!

Grimm's Fairy Tales, 1903.

Illustrated by Helen Stratton

ASCHENPUTTEL

(A German Tale)

Aschenputtel is a German tale written by the Brothers Grimm, (or *Die Brüder Grimm*), Jacob (1785–1863) and Wilhelm Grimm (1786–1859). It was published in *Kinder und Hausmärchen* ('Children's and Household Tales') in 1812; a pioneering collection of German folklore. The Grimms built their anthology on the conviction that a national identity could be found in popular culture and with the common folk (*Volk*). Their first volumes were highly criticised however, because although they were called 'Children's Tales', they were not regarded as suitable for children, for both their scholarly information and gruesome subject matter.

Although similar in many respects to Perrault's narrative, the Grimm's version is less 'bowdlerised', and there is no fairy-godmother, but a wishing tree that grows on Aschenputtel's grave. In addition, unlike Perrault's version, the father does not seem particularly attached to his daughter, and in fact describes her as his 'first wife's child' and not his own.

$$\longrightarrow$$

The wife of a rich man fell sick, and as she felt that her end was drawing near, she called her only daughter to her bedside and said, "Dear child, be good and pious, and then the good God will always protect thee, and I will look down on thee from heaven and be near thee." Thereupon she closed her eyes and departed. Every day the maiden went out to her mother's grave, and wept, and she remained pious and good. When winter came the snow spread a white sheet over the grave, and when the spring sun had drawn it off again, the man had taken another wife.

The woman had brought two daughters into the house with her, who were beautiful and fair of face, but vile and black of heart. Now began a bad time for the poor step-child. "Is the stupid goose to sit in the parlour with us?" said they. "He who wants to eat bread must earn it; out with the kitchen-wench." They took her pretty clothes away from her, put an old grey bed-gown on her, and gave her wooden shoes. "Just look at the proud princess, how decked out she is!" they cried, and laughed, and led her into the kitchen. There she had to do hard work from morning till night, get up before daybreak, carry water, light fires, cook and wash. Besides this, the sisters did her every imaginable injury -- they mocked her and emptied her peas and lentils into the ashes, so that she was forced to sit and pick them out again. In the evening when she had worked till she was weary she had no bed to go to, but had to sleep by the fireside in the ashes. And as on that account she always looked dusty and dirty, they called her Cinderella. It happened that the father was once going to the fair, and he asked his two step-daughters what he should bring back for them. "Beautiful dresses," said one, "Pearls and jewels," said the second. "And thou, Cinderella," said he, "what wilt thou have?" "Father, break off for me the first branch which knocks against your hat on your way home." So he bought beautiful dresses, pearls and jewels for his two step-daughters, and on his way home, as he was riding through a green thicket, a hazel twig brushed against him and knocked off his hat. Then he broke off the branch and took it with him. When he reached home he gave his step-daughters the things which they had wished for, and to Cinderella he gave the branch from the hazel-bush. Cinderella thanked him, went to her mother's grave and planted the branch on it, and wept so much that the tears fell down on it and watered it. And it grew, however, and became a handsome tree. Thrice a day Cinderella went and sat beneath it, and wept and prayed, and a little white bird always came on the tree, and if Cinderella expressed a wish, the bird threw down to her what she had wished for.

The bird threw down a beautiful silk dress.
Grimm's Fairy Tales, 1909.
Illustrated by Millicent Sowerby

"There," said her godmother, pointing with her wand, . . ."pick it and bring it along."
Edmund Dulac's Picture-Book For The French Red Cross, 1915.
Illustrated by Edmund Dulac

It happened, however, that the King appointed a festival which was to last three days, and to which all the beautiful young girls in the country were invited, in order that his son might choose himself a bride. When the two step-sisters heard that they too were to appear among the number, they were delighted, called Cinderella and said, "Comb our hair for us, brush our shoes and fasten our buckles, for we are going to the festival at the King's palace." Cinderella obeyed, but wept, because she too would have liked to go with them to the dance, and begged her step-mother to allow her to do so. "Thou go, Cinderella!" said she; "Thou art dusty and dirty and wouldst go to the festival? Thou hast no clothes and shoes, and yet wouldst dance!" As, however, Cinderella went on asking, the step-mother at last said, "I have emptied a dish of lentils into the ashes for thee, if thou hast picked them out again in two hours, thou shalt go with us." The maiden went through the back-door into the garden, and called, "You tame pigeons, you turtle-doves, and all you birds beneath the sky, come and help me to pick

"The good into the pot,
The bad into the crop."

Then two white pigeons came in by the kitchen-window, and afterwards the turtle-doves, and at last all the birds beneath the sky, came whirring and crowding in, and alighted amongst the ashes. And the pigeons nodded with their heads and began pick, pick, pick, pick, and the rest began also pick, pick, pick, pick, and gathered all the good grains into the dish. Hardly had one hour passed before they had finished, and all flew out again. Then the girl took the dish to her step-mother, and was glad, and believed that now she would be allowed to go with them to the festival. But the step-mother said, "No, Cinderella, thou hast no clothes and thou canst not dance; thou wouldst only be laughed at." And as Cinderella wept at this, the step-mother said, "If thou canst pick two dishes of lentils out of the ashes for me in one hour, thou shalt go with us." And she thought to herself, "That she most certainly cannot do." When the step-mother had emptied the two dishes of lentils amongst the ashes, the maiden went through the back-door into the garden and cried, You tame pigeons, you turtle-doves, and all you birds under heaven, come and help me to pick

> "The good into the pot,
> The bad into the crop."

Then two white pigeons came in by the kitchen-window, and afterwards the turtle-doves, and at length all the birds beneath the sky, came whirring and crowding in, and alighted amongst the ashes. And the doves nodded with their heads and began pick, pick, pick, pick, and the others began also pick, pick, pick, pick, and gathered all the good seeds into the dishes, and before half an hour was over they had already finished, and all flew out again. Then the maiden carried the dishes to the step-mother and was delighted, and believed that she might now go with them to the festival. But the step-mother said, "All this will not help thee; thou goest not with us, for thou hast no clothes and canst not dance; we should be ashamed of thee!" On this she turned her back on Cinderella, and hurried away with her two proud daughters.

As no one was now at home, Cinderella went to her mother's grave beneath the hazel-tree, and cried,

> "Shiver and quiver, little tree,
> Silver and gold throw down over me."

Then the bird threw a gold and silver dress down to her, and slippers embroidered with silk and silver. She put on the dress with all speed, and went to the festival. Her step-sisters and the step-mother however did not know her, and thought she must be a foreign princess, for she looked so beautiful in the golden dress.

She wondered how a pumpkin could help her get to the ball.

Perrault's Fairy Tales, 1867.

Illustrated by Gustave Dore

Cinderella and the Fairy God Mother.
Fairy Tales, 1915.
Illustrated by Margaret Tarrant

They never once thought of Cinderella, and believed that she was sitting at home in the dirt, picking lentils out of the ashes. The prince went to meet her, took her by the hand and danced with her. He would dance with no other maiden, and never left loose of her hand, and if any one else came to invite her, he said, "This is my partner."

She danced till it was evening, and then she wanted to go home. But the King's son said, "I will go with thee and bear thee company," for he wished to see to whom the beautiful maiden belonged. She escaped from him, however, and sprang into the pigeon-house. The King's son waited until her father came, and then he told him that the stranger maiden had leapt into the pigeon-house. The old man thought, "Can it be Cinderella?" and they had to bring him an axe and a pickaxe that he might hew the pigeon-house to pieces, but no one was inside it. And when they got home Cinderella lay in her dirty clothes among the ashes, and a dim little oil-lamp was burning on the mantle-piece, for Cinderella had jumped quickly down from the back of the pigeon-house and had run to the little hazel-tree, and there she had taken off her beautiful clothes and laid them on the grave, and the bird had taken them away again, and then she had placed herself in the kitchen amongst the ashes in her grey gown.

Next day when the festival began afresh, and her parents and the step-sisters had gone once more, Cinderella went to the hazel-tree and said --

> "Shiver and quiver, my little tree,
> Silver and gold throw down over me."

Then the bird threw down a much more beautiful dress than on the preceding day. And when Cinderella appeared at the festival in this dress, every one was astonished at her beauty. The King's son had waited until she came, and instantly took her by the hand and danced with no one but her. When others came and invited her, he said, "She is my partner." When evening came she wished to leave, and the King's son followed her and wanted to see into which house she went. But she sprang away from him, and into the garden behind the house. Therein stood a beautiful tall tree on which hung the most magnificent pears. She clambered so nimbly between the branches like a squirrel that the King's son did not know where she was gone. He waited until her father came, and said to him, "The stranger-maiden has escaped from me, and I believe she has climbed up the pear-tree." The father thought, "Can it be Cinderella?" and had an axe brought and cut the tree down, but no one was on it. And when they got into the kitchen, Cinderella lay there amongst the ashes, as usual, for she had jumped down on the other side of the tree, had taken the beautiful dress to the bird on the little hazel-tree, and put on her grey gown.

On the third day, when the parents and sisters had gone away, Cinderella went once more to her mother's grave and said to the little tree --

"Shiver and quiver, my little tree,
Silver and gold throw down over me."

And now the bird threw down to her a dress which was more splendid and magnificent than any she had yet had, and the slippers were golden. And when she went to the festival in the dress, no one knew how to speak for astonishment. The King's son danced with her only, and if any one invited her to dance, he said, "She is my partner."

When evening came, Cinderella wished to leave, and the King's son was anxious to go with her, but she escaped from him so quickly that he could not follow her. The King's son had, however, used a stratagem, and had caused the whole staircase to be smeared with pitch, and there, when she ran down, had the maiden's left slipper remained sticking. The King's son picked it up, and it was small and dainty, and all golden. Next morning, he went with it to

Now, Cinderella, you may go; but remember…
The Arthur Rackham Fairy Book, 1933.
Illustrated by Arthur Rackham

the father, and said to him, "No one shall be my wife but she whose foot this golden slipper fits." Then were the two sisters glad, for they had pretty feet. The eldest went with the shoe into her room and wanted to try it on, and her mother stood by. But she could not get her big toe into it, and the shoe was too small for her. Then her mother gave her a knife and said, "Cut the toe off; when thou art Queen thou wilt have no more need to go on foot." The maiden cut the toe off, forced the foot into the shoe, swallowed the pain, and went out to the King's son. Then he took her on his horse as his bride and rode away with her. They were, however, obliged to pass the grave, and there, on the hazel-tree, sat the two pigeons and cried,

> "Turn and peep, turn and peep,
> There's blood within the shoe,
> The shoe it is too small for her,
> The true bride waits for you."

Then he looked at her foot and saw how the blood was streaming from it. He turned his horse round and took the false bride home again, and said she was not the true one, and that the other sister was to put the shoe on. Then this one went into her chamber and got her toes safely into the shoe, but her heel was too large. So her mother gave her a knife and said, "Cut a bit off thy heel; when thou art Queen thou wilt have no more need to go on foot." The maiden cut a bit off her heel, forced her foot into the shoe, swallowed the pain, and went out to the King's son. He took her on his horse as his bride, and rode away with her, but when they passed by the hazel-tree, two little pigeons sat on it and cried,

> "Turn and peep, turn and peep,
> There's blood within the shoe
> The shoe it is too small for her,
> The true bride waits for you."

Now, Cinderella, here's your coach to take you to the ball.
The Cinderella Picture Book, 1875.
Illustrated by Walter Crane

Away she drove, scarce able to contain herself for joy.

The Fairy Tales of Charles Perrault, 1922.

Illustrated by Harry Clarke

He looked down at her foot and saw how the blood was running out of her shoe, and how it had stained her white stocking. Then he turned his horse and took the false bride home again. "This also is not the right one," said he, "have you no other daughter?" "No," said the man, "There is still a little stunted kitchen-wench which my late wife left behind her, but she cannot possibly be the bride." The King's son said he was to send her up to him; but the mother answered, "Oh, no, she is much too dirty, she cannot show herself." He absolutely insisted on it, and Cinderella had to be called. She first washed her hands and face clean, and then went and bowed down before the King's son, who gave her the golden shoe. Then she seated herself on a stool, drew her foot out of the heavy wooden shoe, and put it into the slipper, which fitted like a glove. And when she rose up and the King's son looked at her face he recognized the beautiful maiden who had danced with him and cried, "That is the true bride!" The step-mother and the two sisters were terrified and became pale with rage; he, however, took Cinderella on his horse and rode away with her. As they passed by the hazel-tree, the two white doves cried --

"Turn and peep, turn and peep,
No blood is in the shoe,
The shoe is not too small for her,
The true bride rides with you,"

and when they had cried that, the two came flying down and placed themselves on Cinderella's shoulders, one on the right, the other on the left, and remained sitting there.

When the wedding with the King's son had to be celebrated, the two false sisters came and wanted to get into favour with Cinderella and share her good fortune. When the betrothed couple went to church, the elder was at the right side and the younger at the left, and the pigeons pecked out one eye of each of them. Afterwards as they came back, the elder was at the left, and the younger at the right, and then the pigeons pecked out the other eye of each. And thus, for their wickedness and falsehood, they were punished with blindness as long as they lived.

The Kings son gave her his hand.
Tales of Passed Times, 1900.
Illustrated by Charles Robinson

Cinderella appears at the ball.
The Big Book of Fairy Tales, 1911.
Illustrated by Charles Robinson

Sodewa Bai

(A Southern Indian Tale)

This tale was first translated into English by Mary Eliza Isabella Frere (1845 - 1911), a British author who published many works to do with the Indian continent. Frere's book, *Old Deccan Days; or, Hindoo Fairy Legends Current in Southern India. Collected From Oral Tradition* (1868), was the first English-language field-collection of Indian chronicles. According to Frere's introduction, she began her collection during long travels with her father.

Frere's anthology was highly influential, and in a review by the German orientologist Max Müller, was praised for its rendition of Sanskrit reading 'like a direct translation of the ancient language.' In this tale, a princess named Sodewa Bai is born with a golden necklace about her neck, a necklace which contains her soul. In a similar manner to the tale of Rhodopis, Sodewa Bai's lost slipper is also found by a Prince, who thereafter embarks on a grand search.

⇒

Long, long while ago there lived a Rajah and Ranee, who had one only daughter, and she was the most beautiful Princess in the world. Her face was as fair and delicate as the clear moonlight, and they called her Sodewa Bai. At her birth her father and mother had sent for all the wise men in the kingdom to tell her fortune, and they predicted that she would grow up richer and more fortunate than any other lady - and so it was; for, from her earliest youth, she

Ashenputtel goes to the ball.
The Fairy Tales of the Brothers Grimm, 1909.
Illustrated by Arthur Rackham

was good and lovely, and whenever she opened her lips to speak, pearls and precious stones fell upon the ground, and as she walked along they would scatter on either side of her path, insomuch that her father soon became the richest Rajah in all that country - for his daughter could not go across the room without shaking down jewels worth a dowry. Moreover, Sodewa Bai was born with a golden necklace about her neck, concerning which also her parents consulted astrologers, who said, 'This is no common child; the necklace of gold about her neck contains your daughter's soul; let it therefore be guarded with the utmost care; for if it were taken off, and worn by another person, she would die.' So the Ranee, her mother, caused it to be firmly fastened round the child's neck, and as soon as she was old enough to understand, instructed her concerning its value, and bade her on no account ever allow it to be taken off.

At the time my story begins, this Princess was fourteen years old; but she was not married, for her father and mother had promised that she should not do so until it pleased herself; and although many great rajahs and nobles sought her hand, she constantly refused them all.

Now Sodewa Bai's father, on one of her birthdays, gave her a lovely pair of slippers, made of gold and jewels. Each slipper was worth a hundred thousand gold mohurs. There were none like them in all the earth. Sodewa Bai prized these slippers very much, and always wore them when she went out walking, to protect her tender feet from the stones; but one day, as she was wandering with her ladies upon the side of the mountain on which the palace was built, playing, and picking the wild-flowers, her foot slipped and one of the golden slippers fell down, down, down the steep hill-slope, over rocks and stones, into the jungle below. Sodewa Bai sent attendants to search for it, and the Rajah caused criers to go throughout the town and proclaim that whoever discovered the Princess's slipper should receive a great reward; but though it was hunted for far and near, high and low, it could not be found.

It chanced, however, that not very long after this, a young Prince, the eldest son of a Rajah who lived in the plains, was out hunting, and in the jungle he picked up the very little golden slipper which Sodewa Bai had lost, and which had tumbled all the way from the mountain-side into the depths of the forest. He took it home with him, and showed it to his mother, saying, 'What a fairy foot must have worn this tiny slipper!'--'Ah, my boy,' she said, 'this must in truth have belonged to a lovely Princess; (if she is but as beautiful as her slipper!) would that you could find such a one to be your wife!' Then they sent into all the towns of the kingdom, to inquire for the owner of the lost slipper; but she could not be found. At last, when many months had gone by, it happened that news was brought by travellers to the Rajah's capital of how, in a far-distant land, very high among the mountains, there lived a beautiful Princess who had lost her slipper, and whose father had offered a great reward to whoever should restore it; and from the description they gave, all were assured it was the one that the Prince had found.

Then his mother said to him, 'My son, it is certain that the slipper you found belongs to none other than the great Mountain Rajah's daughter; therefore take it to his palace, and when he offers you the promised reward, say that you wish for neither silver nor gold, but ask him to give you his daughter in marriage. Thus you may gain her for your wife.'

The Prlnce did as his mother advised; and when, after a long, long Journey, he reached the court of Sodewa Bai's father, he presented the Slipper to him, saying, 'I have found your daughter's slipper, and, for restoring it, I claim a great reward.'-- 'What will you have? said the Rajah. 'Shall I pay you in horses? or in silver? or gold?'-- 'No,' answered the Prince, 'I will have none of these things. I am the son of a Rajah who lives in the plains, and I found this slipper in the jungle where I was hunting, and have travelled for many weary days to bring it you; but the only payment I care for is the hand of your beautiful daughter; if it pleases you, let me become your son-in-law.' The Rajah replied,

Cendrillon and the Prince.
Contes de Perrault, 1910.
Illustrated by Margaret Tarrant

All the evening her never left her side.
Cinderella - Retold by C. S. Evans, 1909.
Illustrated by Arthur Rackham

'This only I cannot promise you; for I have vowed I will not oblige my daughter to marry against her will. This matter depends upon her alone. If she is willing to be your wife, I also am willing; but it rests with her free choice.'

Now it happened that Sodewa Bai had from her window seen the prince coming up to the palace gate, and when she heard his errand, she said to her father, 'I saw that Prince, and I am willing to marry him.'

So they Were married with great pomp and splendour.

When, however, all the other Rajahs, Sodewa Bai's suitors, heard of her choice, they were much astonished, as well as vexed, and said, 'What can have made Sodewa Bai take a fancy to that young Prince? He is not so wonderfully handsome, and he is very poor. This is a most foolish marriage.' But they all came to it, and were entertained at the palace, where the wedding festivities lasted many days.

After Sodewa Bai and her husband had lived there for some little time, he one day said to his father-in-law, 'I have a great desire to see my own people again, and to return to my own country. Let me take my wife home with me.' The Rajah said, 'Very well I am willing that you should go. Take care of your wife; guard her as the apple of your eye; and be sure you never permit the golden necklace to be taken from her neck and given to any one else, for in that case she would die.' The Prince promised; and he returned with Sodewa Bai to his father's kingdom. At their departure the Rajah of the Mountain gave them many elephants, horses, camels, and attendants, besides jewels innumerable, and much money, and many rich hangings, robes, and carpets. The old Rajah and Ranee of the Plain were delighted to welcome home their son and his beautiful bride; and there they might all have lived their lives long in uninterrupted peace and happiness, had it not been for one unfortunate circumstance. Rowjee (for that was the Prince's name) had another wife, to whom he had been married when a child, long before he found Sodewa Bai's golden slipper; she, therefore, was the first Ranee, though Sodewa Bai was the one he loved the best (for the first Ranee was of a sullen, morose, and jealous disposition). His father, also, and his mother, preferred Sodewa Bai to their other daughter-in-law. The first Ranee could not bear to think of any one being Ranee beside herself; and more especially of another, not only in the same position, but better loved by all around than she; and therefore, in her wicked heart, she hated Sodewa Bai and longed for her destruction, though outwardly pretending to be very fond of her. The old Rajah and Ranee, knowing the first Ranee's jealous and envious disposition, never liked Sodewa Bai to be much with her; but as they had only a vague fear, and no certain ground for alarm, they could do no more than watch both carefully; and Sodewa Bai, who was guileless and unsuspicious, would remonstrate with them when they warned her not to be so intimate with Rowjee Rajah's other wife, saying, 'I have no fear. I think she loves me as I love her. Why should we disagree? Are we not sisters?' One day, Rowjee Rajah was obliged to go on a journey to a distant part of his father's kingdom, and being unable to take Sodewa Bai with him, he left her in his parents' charge, promising to return soon, and begging them to watch over her, and to go every morning and see that she was well; which they agreed to do.

A little while after their husband had gone, the first Ranee went to Sodewa Bai's room and said to her, 'It is lonely for us both, now Rowjee is away; but you must come often to see me, and I will come often to see you and talk to you, and so we will amuse ourselves as well as we can.' To this Sodewa Bai agreed; and to amuse the first Ranee she took out all her jewels and pretty things to show her. As they were looking over them, the first Ranee said, 'I notice you always wear that row of golden beads round your neck. Why do you? Have you any reason for always wearing the same ones?' -- 'Oh yes,' answered Sodewa Bai thoughtlessly. 'I was born with these beads round my neck, and the wise men told my father and mother that they contain my soul,

Whereupon she instantly desired her partner to lead her to the King and Lueen.
The Sleeping Beauty and Other Fairy Tales From the Old French, 1910.
Illustrated by Edmund Dulac

and that if any one else wore them I should die. So I always wear them. I have never once taken them off.' When the first Ranee heard this news, she was very pleased; yet she feared to steal the beads herself, both because she was afraid she might be found out, and because she did not like with her own hands to commit the crime. So, returning to her house, she called her most confidential servant, a negress, whom she knew to be trustworthy, and said to her, 'Go this evening to Sodewa Bai's room, when she is asleep, and take from her neck the string of golden beads, fasten them round your own neck, and return to me. Those beads contain her soul, and as soon as you put them on, she will cease to live.' The negress agreed to do as she was told; for she had long known that her mistress hated Sodewa Bai, and desired nothing so much as her death. So that night, going softly into the sleeping Ranee's room, she stole the golden necklace, and, fastening it round her own neck, crept away without any one knowing what was done; and when the negress put on the necklace, Sodewa Bai's spirit fled.

Next morning the old Rajah and Ranee went as usual to see their daughter-in-law, and knocked at the door of her room. No one answered. They knocked again, and again; still no reply. They then went in, and found her lying there, cold as marble, and quite dead, though she had seemed very well when they saw her only the day before. They asked her attendants, who slept just outside her door, whether she had been ill that night, or if any one had gone into her room? But they declared they had heard no sound, and were sure no one had been near the place. In vain the Rajah and Ranee sent for the most learned doctors in the kingdom, to see if there was still any spark of life remaining; all said that the young Ranee was dead, beyond reach of hope or help.

Then the Rajah and Ranee were very grieved, and mourned bitterly; and because they desired that, if possible, Rowjee Rajah should see his wife once again, instead of burying her under ground, they placed her beneath a canopy in a beautiful tomb near a little tank, and would go daily to visit the place

Cinderella.
My Book of Favourite Fairy Tales, 1921.
Illustrated by Jennie Harbour

Straight out of the ball-room she scampered down the marble staircase.
Told Again - Old Tales Told Again, 1927.
Illustrated by A. H. Watson

and look at her. Then did a wonder take place, such as had never been known throughout the land before! Sodewa Bai's body did not decay, nor the colour of her face change; and a month afterwards, when her husband returned home, she looked as fair and lovely as on the night on which she died. There was a fresh colour in her cheeks and on her lips; she seemed to be only asleep. When poor Rowjee Rajah heard of her death, he was so broken-hearted they thought he also would die. He cursed the evil fate that had deprived him of hearing her last words, or bidding her farewell, if he could not save her life; and from morning to evening he would go to her tomb and rend the air with his passionate lamentations, and looking through the grating to where she lay calm and still under the canopy, say, before he went away, 'I will take one last look at that fair face. To-morrow Death may have set his seal upon it. O loveliness too bright for earth! O lost, lost wife!'

The Rajah and Ranee feared that he would die, or go mad, and they tried to prevent his going to the tomb; but all was of no avail; it seemed to be the only thing he cared for in life.

Now the negress who had stolen Sodewa Bai's necklace used to wear it all day long, but late each night, on going to bed, she would take it off, and put it by till next morning, and whenever she took it off Sodewa Bai's spirit returned to her again, and she lived till day dawned and the negress put on the necklace, when she again died. But as the tomb was far from any houses, and the old Rajah and Ranee, and Rowjee Rajah, only went there by day, nobody found this out. When Sodewa Bai first came to life in this way she felt very frightened to find herself there all alone in the dark, and thought she was in prison; but afterwards she got more accustomed to it, and determined when morning came to look about the place, and find her way back to the palace, and recover the necklace she found she had lost (for it would have been dangerous to go at night through the jungles that surrounded the tomb, where she could hear the wild beasts roaring all night long); but morning never came, for whenever the

Ashputtel.

Grimm's Household Tales, 1936.

Illustrated by R. Anning Bell

negress awoke and put on the golden beads Sodewa Bai died. However, each night, when the Ranee came to life, she would walk to the little tank by the tomb, and drink some of the cool water, and return; but food she had none. Now no pearls or precious stones fell from her lips, because she had no one to talk to; but each time she walked down to the tank she scattered jewels on either side of her path; and one day, when Rowjee Rajah went to the tomb, he noticed all these jewels, and thinking it very strange (though he never dreamed that his wife could come to life), determined to watch and see whence they came. But although he watched and waited long, he could not find out the cause, because all day Sodewa Bai lay still and dead, and only came to life at night. It was just at this time, two whole months after she had been buried, and the night after the very day that Rowjee Rajah had spent in watching by the tomb, that Sodewa Bai had a little son; but directly after he was born, day dawned, and the mother died. The little lonely baby began to cry, but no one was there to hear him; and, as it chanced, the Rajah did not go to the tomb that day, for he thought, 'All yesterday I watched by the tomb and saw nothing; instead, therefore, of going to-day, I will wait till the evening, and then see again if I cannot find out how the jewels came there.'

So at night he went to the place. When he got there he heard a faint cry from inside the tomb; but what it was he knew not; perhaps it might be a Pen, or an evil spirit. As he was wondering, the door opened, and Sodewa Bai crossed the courtyard to the tank with a child in her arms, and as she walked showers of jewels fell on both sides of her path. Rowjee Rajah thought he must be in a dream; but when he saw the Ranee drink some water from the tank and return towards the tomb, he sprang up and hurried after her. Sodewa Bai, hearing footsteps follow her, was frightened, and running into the tomb, fastened the door. Then the Rajah knocked at it, saying, 'Let me in; let me in.' She answered, 'Who are you? Are you a Rakshas, or a spirit?' (For she thought, 'Perhaps this is some cruel creature who will kill me and the child.') 'No, no,' cried the Rajah, 'I am no Rakshas, but your husband. Let me in, Sodewa Bai, if you are indeed alive.' No sooner did he name her name than Sodewa Bai knew his voice, and unbolted the door and let him in. Then, when he saw her sitting on the tomb with the baby on her lap, he fell down on his knees before her, saying, 'Tell me, little wife, that this is not a dream.'--'No,' she answered, 'I am indeed alive, and this our child was born last night; but every day I die; for while you were away some one stole my golden necklace.'

Then for the first time Rowjee Rajah noticed that the beads were no longer round her neck. So he bade her fear nothing, for that he would assuredly recover them and return; and going back to the palace, which he reached in the early morning, he summoned before him the whole household.

Then, upon the neck of the negress, servant to the first Ranee, he saw Sodewa Bai's missing necklace, and seizing it, ordered his guards to take the woman to prison. The negress, frightened, confessed that all she had done was by the first Ranee's order, and how, at her command, she had stolen the necklace. And when the Rajah learnt this, he ordered that the first Ranee also should be imprisoned for life; and he and his father and mother all went together to the tomb, and placing the lost beads round Sodewa's Bai's neck, brought her and the child back in triumph with them to the palace. Then, at news of how the young Ranee had been restored to life, there was great joy throughout all that country, and many days were spent in rejoicings in honour of that happy event; and for the rest of their lives the old Rajah and Ranee, and Rowjee Rajah and Sodewa Bai, and all the family, lived in health and happiness.

The Soldier Lays a Honey Trap.
European Folk and Fairy Tales, 1916.
Illustrated by John D. Batten

She sprang away from him all at once, into the garden behind her fathers house.
My Book of Favourite Fairy Tales, 1921.
Illustrated by Jennie Harbour

THE WONDERFUL BIRCH

(A Finnish/Russian Tale)

The Wonderful Birch is a folkloric narrative of Finland and Russia. It was first written down by the Scottish folklorist Andrew Lang (1844 - 1912), in *The Red Fairy Book* (1890). Lang produced twelve collections of fairy tales in total, each volume distinguished by its own colour. Although he did not collect the stories himself from oral primary sources, Lang is only rivalled by Madame d'Aulnoy (1650 - 1705) for the sheer variety of sources and cultural diversity included in his anthologies.

The Wonderful Birch makes much use of shape-shifting motifs. In this narrative, an evil witch captures the mother, assumes her form, turns her into a sheep and kills her – feeding the meat to the father. However the young daughter ('Cinder Wench') refuses to eat the meat and buries her mother's bones. They grow into a beautiful birch tree. Later, the witch sets 'Cinder Wench' a series of impossible tasks, which the girl manages to complete with the aid of the magical birch tree.

$$\longrightarrow$$

Once upon a time there were a man and a woman, who had an only daughter. Now it happened that one of their sheep went astray, and they set out to look for it, and searched and searched, each in a different part of the wood. Then the good wife met a witch, who said to her, "If you spit, you miserable creature, if you spit into the sheath of my knife, or if you run between my legs, I shall change you into a black sheep."

The woman neither spat, nor did she run between her legs, but yet the witch changed her into a sheep. Then she made herself look exactly like the woman, and called out to the good man, "Ho, old man, halloa! I have found the sheep already!"

The man thought the witch was really his wife, and he did not know that his wife was the sheep; so he went home with her, glad at heart because his sheep was found. When they were safe at home the witch said to the man, "Look here, old man, we must really kill that sheep lest it run away to the wood again."

The man, who was a peaceable quiet sort of fellow, made no objections, but simply said, "Good, let us do so."

The daughter, however, had overheard their talk, and she ran to the flock and lamented aloud, "Oh, dear little mother, they are going to slaughter you!"

"Well, then, if they do slaughter me," was the black sheep's answer, "eat you neither the meat nor the broth that is made of me, but gather all my bones, and bury them by the edge of the field."

Shortly after this they took the black sheep from the flock and slaughtered it. The witch made pease-soup of it, and set it before the daughter. But the girl remembered her mother's warning.

She did not touch the soup, but she carried the bones to the edge of the field and buried them there; and there sprang up on the spot a birch tree -- a very lovely birch tree.

Some time had passed away -- who can tell how long they might have been living there? -- when the witch, to whom a child had been born in the

Cinderella's Flight.
The Blue Fairy Book, 1898.
Illustrated by G. P. Jacomb Hood

meantime, began to take an ill-will to the man's daughter, and to torment her in all sorts of ways.

Now it happened that a great festival was to be held at the palace, and the king had commanded that all the people should be invited, and that this proclamation should be made:

"Come, people all!
Poor and wretched, one and all!
Blind and crippled though ye be,
Mount your steeds or come by sea."

And so they drove into the king's feast all the outcasts, and the maimed, and the halt, and the blind. In the good man's house, too, preparations were made to go to the palace. The witch said to the man, "Go you on in front, old man, with our youngest; I will give the elder girl work to keep her from being dull in our absence."

So the man took the child and set out. But the witch kindled a fire on the hearth, threw a potful of barleycorns among the cinders, and said to the girl, "If you have not picked the barley out of the ashes, and put it all back in the pot before nightfall, I shall eat you up!"

Then she hastened after the others, and the poor girl stayed at home and wept. She tried to be sure to pick up the grains of barley, but she soon saw how useless her labor was; and so she went in her sore trouble to the birch tree on her mother's grave, and cried and cried, because her mother lay dead beneath the sod and could help her no longer. In the midst of her grief she suddenly heard her mother's voice speak from the grave, and say to her, "Why do you weep, little daughter?"

As Cinderella left the ball-room one of her glass slippers fell off.
Fairy Tales, 1915.
Illustrated by Margaret Tarrant

Cinderella and the Glass Slipper.
Old, Old Fairy Tales, 1935.
Illustrated by Anne Anderson

"The witch has scattered barleycorns on the hearth, and bid me pick them out of the ashes," said the girl; "that is why I weep, dear little mother."

"Do not weep," said her mother consolingly. "Break off one of my branches, and strike the hearth with it crosswise, and all will be put right."

The girl did so. She struck the hearth with the birchen branch, and lo! the barleycorns flew into the pot, and the hearth was clean. Then she went back to the birch tree and laid the branch upon the grave. Then her mother bade her bathe on one side of the stem, dry herself on another, and dress on the third. When the girl had done all that, she had grown so lovely that no one on earth could rival her. Splendid clothing was given to her, and a horse, with hair partly of gold, partly of silver, and partly of something more precious still. The girl sprang into the saddle, and rode as swift as an arrow to the palace.

As she turned into the courtyard of the castle the king's son came out to meet her, tied her steed to a pillar, and led her in. He never left her side as they passed through the castle rooms; and all the people gazed at her, and wondered who the lovely maiden was, and from what castle she came; but no one knew her - no one knew anything about her. At the banquet the prince invited her to sit next him in the place of honour; but the witch's daughter gnawed the bones under the table. The prince did not see her, and thinking it was a dog, he gave her such a push with his foot that her arm was broken. Are you not sorry for the witch's daughter? It was not her fault that her mother was a witch.

Towards evening the good man's daughter thought it was time to go home; but as she went, her ring caught on the latch of the door, for the king's son had had it smeared with tar. She did not take time to pull it off, but, hastily unfastening her horse from the pillar, she rode away beyond the castle walls as swift as an arrow. Arrived at home, she took off her clothes by the birch tree, left her horse standing there, and hastened to her place behind the stove. In a

She left behind one of her glass slippers, which the Prince took up most carefully.
The Fairy Tales of Charles Perrault, 1922.
Illustrated by Harry Clarke

short time the man and the woman came home again too, and the witch said to the girl, "Ah! you poor thing, there you are to be sure! You don't know what fine times we have had at the palace! The king's son carried my daughter about, but the poor thing fell and broke her arm."

The girl knew well how matters really stood, but she pretended to know nothing about it, and sat dumb behind the stove.

The next day they were invited again to the king's banquet.

"Hey! old man," said the witch, "get on your clothes as quick as you can; we are bidden to the feast. Take you the child; I will give the other one work, lest she weary."

She kindled the fire, threw a potful of hemp seed among the ashes, and said to the girl, "If you do not get this sorted, and all the seed back into the pot, I shall kill you!"

The girl wept bitterly; then she went to the birch tree, washed herself on one side of it and dried herself on the other; and this time still finer clothes were given to her, and a very beautiful steed. She broke off a branch of the birch tree, struck the hearth with it, so that the seeds flew into the pot, and then hastened to the castle.

Again the king's son came out to meet her, tied her horse to a pillar, and led her into the banqueting hall. At the feast the girl sat next him in the place of honor, as she had done the day before. But the witch's daughter gnawed bones under the table, and the prince gave her a push by mistake, which broke her leg - he had never noticed her crawling about among the people's feet. She was very unlucky!

The good man's daughter hastened home again betimes, but the king's son had smeared the door-posts with tar, and the girl's golden circlet stuck to it. She had not time to look for it, but sprang to the saddle and rode like an arrow to the birch tree. There she left her horse and her fine clothes, and said to her mother, "I have lost my circlet at the castle; the door-post was tarred, and it stuck fast."

"And even had you lost two of them," answered her mother, "I would give you finer ones."

Then the girl hastened home, and when her father came home from the feast with the witch, she was in her usual place behind the stove. Then the witch said to her, "You poor thing! what is there to see here compared with what we have seen at the palace? The king's son carried my daughter from one room to another; he let her fall, 'tis true, and my child's foot was broken."

The man's daughter held her peace all the time, and busied herself about the hearth.

The night passed, and when the day began to dawn, the witch awakened her husband, crying, "Hi! get up, old man! We are bidden to the royal banquet."

So the old man got up. Then the witch gave him the child, saying, "Take you the little one; I will give the other girl work to do, else she will weary at home alone."

She did as usual. This time it was a dish of milk she poured upon the ashes, saying, "If you do not get all the milk into the dish again before I come home, you will suffer for it."

Nothing remained of her magnificence save one of her little glass slippers.
Perrault's Fairy Tales, 1913.
Illustrated by Honor Appleton

The only remnant of her past magnificence being one of her little glass slippers.
The Fairy Book, 1923.
Illustrated by Warwick Goble

How frightened the girl was this time! She ran to the birch tree, and by its magic power her task was accomplished; and then she rode away to the palace as before. When she got to the courtyard she found the prince waiting for her. He led her into the hall, where she was highly honored; but the witch's daughter sucked the bones under the table, and crouching at the people's feet she got an eye knocked out, poor thing! Now no one knew any more than before about the good man's daughter, no one knew whence she came; but the prince had had the threshold smeared with tar, and as she fled her gold slippers stuck to it. She reached the birch tree, and laying aside her finery, she said, "Alas I dear little mother, I have lost my gold slippers!"

"Let them be," was her mother's reply; "if you need them I shall give you finer ones."

Scarcely was she in her usual place behind the stove when her father came home with the witch. Immediately the witch began to mock her, saying, "Ah! you poor thing, there is nothing for you to see here, and we -- ah! what great things we have seen at the palace! My little girl was carried about again, but had the ill-luck to fall and get her eye knocked out. You stupid thing, you, what do you know about anything?"

"Yes, indeed, what can I know?" replied the girl; "I had enough to do to get the hearth clean."

Now the prince had kept all the things the girl had lost, and he soon set about finding the owner of them. For this purpose a great banquet was given on the fourth day, and all the people were invited to the palace. The witch got ready to go too. She tied a wooden beetle on where her child's foot should have been, a log of wood instead of an arm, and stuck a bit of dirt in the empty socket for an eye, and took the child with her to the castle. When all the people were gathered together, the king's son stepped in among the crowd and cried,

After that the Prince sent out a proclamation that every lady in the town and in the country round about, be she high or low, must try on the glass slipper.

Cinderella - Retold by C. S. Evans, 1909.

Illustrated by Arthur Rackham

"The maiden whose finger this ring slips over, whose head this golden hoop encircles, and whose foot this shoe fits, shall be my bride."

What a great trying on there was now among them all! The things would fit no one, however.

"The cinder wench is not here," said the prince at last; "go and fetch her, and let her try on the things."

So the girl was fetched, and the prince was just going to hand the ornaments to her, when the witch held him back, saying, "Don't give them to her; she soils everything with cinders; give them to my daughter rather."

Well, then the prince gave the witch's daughter the ring, and the woman filed and pared away at her daughter's finger till the ring fitted. It was the same with the circlet and the shoes of gold. The witch would not allow them to be handed to the cinder wench; she worked at her own daughter's head and feet till she got the things forced on. What was to be done now? The prince had to take the witch's daughter for his bride whether he would or no; he sneaked away to her father's house with her, however, for he was ashamed to hold the wedding festivities at the palace with so strange a bride. Some days passed, and at last he had to take his bride home to the palace, and he got ready to do so. Just as they were taking leave, the kitchen wench sprang down from her place by the stove, on the pretext of fetching something from the cow-house, and in going by she whispered in the prince's ear as he stood in the yard, "Alas! dear prince, do not rob me of my silver and my gold."

Thereupon the king's son recognized the cinder wench; so he took both the girls with him, and set out. After they had gone some little way they came to the bank of a river, and the prince threw the witch's daughter across to serve as a bridge, and so got over with the cinder wench. There lay the witch's daughter then, like a bridge over the river, and could not stir, though her heart was consumed with grief. No help was near, so she cried at last in her anguish, "May there grow a golden hemlock out of my body! perhaps my mother will know me by that token."

Scarcely had she spoken when a golden hemlock sprang up from her, and stood upon the bridge.

Now, as soon as the prince had got rid of the witch's daughter he greeted the cinder wench as his bride, and they wandered together to the birch tree which grew upon the mother's grave. There they received all sorts of treasures and riches, three sacks full of gold, and as much silver, and a splendid steed, which bore them home to the palace. There they lived a long time together, and the young wife bore a son to the prince. Immediately word was brought to the witch that her daughter had borne a son - for they all believed the young king's wife to be the witch's daughter.

"So, so," said the witch to herself; "I had better away with my gift for the infant, then."

And so saying she set out. Thus it happened that she came to the bank of the river, and there she saw the beautiful golden hemlock growing in the middle of the bridge, and when she began to cut it down to take to her grandchild, she heard a voice moaning, "Alas! dear mother, do not cut me so!"

"Are you here?" demanded the witch.

"Indeed I am, dear little mother," answered the daughter "They threw me across the river to make a bridge of me."

The Prime Minister was kept very busy during the next few weeks.
The Sleeping Beauty and Other Fairy Tales From the Old French, 1910.
Illustrated by Edmund Dulac

The step-sister cuts off her toe.

European Folk and Fairy Tales, 1916.

Illustrated by John D. Batten

In a moment the witch had the bridge shivered to atoms, and then she hastened away to the palace. Stepping up to the young Queen's bed, she began to try her magic arts upon her, saying, "Spit, you wretch, on the blade of my knife; bewitch my knife's blade for me, and I shall change you into a reindeer of the forest."

"Are you there again to bring trouble upon me?" said the young woman.

She neither spat nor did anything else, but still the witch changed her into a reindeer, and smuggled her own daughter into her place as the prince's wife. But now the child grew restless and cried, because it missed its mother's care. They took it to the court, and tried to pacify it in every conceivable way, but its crying never ceased.

"What makes the child so restless?" asked the prince, and he went to a wise widow woman to ask her advice.

"Ay, ay, your own wife is not at home," said the widow woman; "she is living like a reindeer in the wood; you have the witch's daughter for a wife now, and the witch herself for a mother-in- law."

"Is there any way of getting my own wife back from the wood again?" asked the prince.

"Give me the child," answered the widow woman. "I'll take it with me tomorrow when I go to drive the cows to the wood. I'll make a rustling among the birch leaves and a trembling among the aspens -- perhaps the boy will grow quiet when he hears it."

"Yes, take the child away, take it to the wood with you to quiet it," said the prince, and led the widow woman into the castle.

"How now? you are going to send the child away to the wood?" said the witch in a suspicious tone, and tried to interfere.

But the king's son stood firm by what he had commanded, and said, "Carry the child about the wood; perhaps that will pacify it."

So the widow woman took the child to the wood. She came to the edge of a marsh, and seeing a herd of reindeer there, she began all at once to sing:

"Little Bright-eyes, little Redskin,
Come nurse the child you bore!
That bloodthirsty monster,
That man-eater grim,
Shall nurse him, shall tend him no more.
They may threaten and force as they will,
He turns from her, shrinks from her still,"

and immediately the reindeer drew near, and nursed and tended the child the whole day long; but at nightfall it had to follow the herd, and said to the widow woman, "Bring me the child tomorrow, and again the following day; after that I must wander with the herd far away to other lands."

The following morning the widow woman went back to the castle to fetch the child. The witch interfered, of course, but the prince said, "Take it, and carry it about in the open air; the boy is quieter at night, to be sure, when he has been in the wood all day."

So the widow took the child in her arms, and carried it to the marsh in the forest. There she sang as on the preceding day:

"Will you please sit down, madam," said he, "and try this slipper on?"
Cinderella - Retold by C. S. Evans, 1909.
Illustrated by Arthur Rackham

"Little Bright-eyes, little Redskin,
Come nurse the child you bore!
That bloodthirsty monster,
That man-eater grim,
Shall nurse him, shall tend him no more.
They may threaten and force as they will,
He turns from her, shrinks from her still,"

and immediately the reindeer left the herd and came to the child, and tended it as on the day before. And so it was that the child throve, till not a finer boy was to be seen anywhere. But the king's son had been pondering over all these things, and he said to the widow woman, "Is there no way of changing the reindeer into a human being again?"

"I don't rightly know," was her answer. "Come to the wood with me, however; when the woman puts off her reindeer skin I shall comb her head for her; whilst I am doing so you must burn the skin."

Thereupon they both went to the wood with the child; scarcely were they there when the reindeer appeared and nursed the child as before. Then the widow woman said to the reindeer, "Since you are going far away tomorrow, and I shall not see you again, let me comb your head for the last time, as a remembrance of you."

Good; the young woman stripped off the reindeer skin, and let the widow woman do as she wished. In the meantime the king's son threw the reindeer skin into the fire unobserved.

"What smells of singeing here?" asked the young woman, and looking round she saw her own husband. "Woe is me! you have burnt my skin. Why did you do that?"

Cinderella and the Glass Slipper.
The Fairy Tales of Charles Perrault, 1922.
Illustrated by Harry Clarke

It went on very easily.

The Tales of Mother Goose, 1901.

Illustrated by D. J. Munro

"To give you back your human form again."

"Alack-a-day! I have nothing to cover me now, poor creature that I am!" cried the young woman, and transformed herself first into a distaff, then into a wooden beetle, then into a spindle, and into all imaginable shapes. But all these shapes the king's son went on destroying till she stood before him in human form again.

"Alas! wherefore take me home with you again," cried the young woman, "since the witch is sure to eat me up?"

"She will not eat you up," answered her husband; and they started for home with the child.

But when the witch wife saw them she ran away with her daughter, and if she has not stopped she is running still, though at a great age. And the prince, and his wife, and the baby lived happy ever afterwards.

Ashputtel put on the golden slipper.
Grimm's Fairy Tales, 1917.
Illustrated by Louis Rhead

RASHIN - COATIE

(A Scottish Tale)

Rashin-Coatie is a Scottish fairy tale collected by Joseph Jacobs (1854 - 1916) in his *More English Fairy Tales* (1894). Jacobs was inspired by the work of the Brothers Grimm and the romantic nationalism common to folklorists of his age; he wished English children to have access to English fairy tales, whereas they were chiefly reading French and German tales. In his own words, 'What Perrault began, the Grimms completed.'

In this variant, the supernatural element takes the form of a red calf (in a similar manner to the ancient Egyptian tale of Rhodopis). The protagonist is the beautiful daughter of a King, but on his re-marriage, she is mistreated by her step-family, who give her far too little food and only a coat made of rushes to wear - calling her 'Rashin-Coatie.' The grizzly lengths the step-sister goes to, in order to 'make the shoe fit' is redolent of much earlier, oral versions of the narrative.

➤———→

Once, a long time ago, there was a gentleman had two lassies. The oldest was ugly and ill natured, but the youngest was a bonnie lassie and good; but the ugly one was the favorite with her father and mother. So they ill used the youngest in every way, and they sent her into the woods to herd cattle, and all the food she got was a little porridge and whey.

Well, amongst the cattle was a red calf, and one day it said to the lassie, "Gee that porridge and whey to the doggie, and come wi' me."

So the lassie followed the calf through the wood, and they came to a bonnie hoosie, where there was a nice dinner ready for them; and after they had feasted on everything nice they went back to the herding.

Every day the calf took the lassie away, and feasted her on dainties; and every day she grew bonnier. This disappointed the father and mother and the ugly sister. They expected that the rough usage she was getting would take away her beauty; and they watched and watched until they saw the calf take the lassie away to the feast. So they resolved to kill the calf; and not only that, but the lassie was to be compelled to kill him with an axe. Her ugly sister was to hold his head, and the lassie who loved him had to give the blow and kill him.

She could do nothing but greet; but the calf told her not to greet, but to do as he bade her; and his plan was that instead of coming down on his head she was to come down on the lassie's head who was holding him, and then she was to jump on his back and they would run off. Well, the day came for the calf to be killed, and everything was ready -- the ugly lassie holding his head, and the bonnie lassie armed with the axe. So she raised the axe, and came down on the ugly sister's head; and in the confusion that took place she got on the calf's back and they ran away. And they ran and better nor ran till they came to a meadow where grew a great lot of rashes; and, as the lassie had not on many clothes, they pu'ed rashes, and made a coatie for her. And they set off again and traveled, and traveled, till they came to the king's house. They went in, and asked if they wanted a servant. The mistress said she wanted a kitchen lassie, and she would take Rashin-Coatie.

So Rashin-Coatie said she would stop, if they keep it the calf too. They were willing to do that. So the lassie and the calf stoppit in the king's house, and everybody was well pleased with her; and when Yule came, they said she was to stop at home and make the dinner, while all the rest went to the kirk. After they were away the calf asked if she would like to go. She said she would,

On Cinderella's dainty little foot the slipper appeared to be a skin of glass.
Fairy Tales, 1915.
Illustrated by Margaret Tarrant

They all threw after them for luck old slippers - not of glass.
The Cinderella Picture Book, 1875.
Illustrated by Walter Crane

but she had no clothes, and she could not leave the dinner. The calf said he would give her clothes, and make the dinner too. He went out, and came back with a grand dress, all silk and satin, and such a nice pair of slippers. The lassie put on the dress, and before she left she said:

> "Ilka peat gar anither burn,
> An' ilka spit gar anither turn,
> An' ilka pot gar anither play,
> Till I come frae the kirk on gude Yule day."

So she went to the kirk, and nobody kent it was Rashin-Coatie. They wondered who the bonnie lady could be; and, as soon as the young prince saw her, he fell in love with her, and resolved he would find out who she was, before she got home; but Rashin-Coatie left before the rest, so that she might get home in time to take off her dress, and look after the dinner.

When the prince saw her leaving, he made for the door to stop her; but she jumped past him, and in the hurry lost one of her shoes. The prince kept the shoe, and Rashin-Coatie got home all right, and the folk said the dinner was very nice.

Now the prince was resolved to find out who the bonnie lady was, and he sent a servant through all the land with the shoe. Every lady was to try it on, and the prince promised to marry the one it would fit. That servant went to a great many houses, but could not find a lady that the shoe would go on, it was so little and neat. At last he came to a henwife's house, and her daughter had little feet. At first the shoe would not go on, but she paret her feet, and clippit her toes, until the shoes went on. Now the prince was very angry. He knew it was not the lady that he wanted; but, because he had promised to marry whoever the shoe fitted, he had to keep his promise.

The marriage day came, and, as they were all riding to the kirk, a little bird flew through the air, and it sang:

> "Clippit feet an' paret taes is on the saidle set;
> But bonnie feet an' braw feet sits in the kitchen neuk."

"What's that ye say?" said the prince

"Oh," says the henwife, "would ye mind what a feel bird says?"

But the prince said, "Sing that again, bonnie birdie."

So the bird sings:

> "Clippit feet an' paret taes is on the saidle set;
> But bonnie feet an' braw feet sits in the kitchen neuk."

The prince turned his horse and rode home, and went straight to his father's kitchen, and there sat Rashin-Coatie. He kent her at once, she was so bonnie; and when she tried on the shoe it fitted her, and so the prince married Rashin-Coatie, and they lived happy, and built a house for the red calf, who had been so kind to her.

Cendrillon.
Les Contes Des Fees, 1908.
Illustrated by M. M. Parquet

The Golden Age of Illustration

The 'Golden age of Illustration' refers to a period customarily defined as lasting from the latter quarter of the nineteenth century until just after the First World War. In this period of no more than fifty years the popularity, abundance and most importantly the unprecedented upsurge in quality of illustrated works marked an astounding change in the way that publishers, artists and the general public came to view this hitherto insufficiently esteemed art form.

Until the latter part of the nineteenth century, the work of illustrators was largely proffered anonymously, and in England it was only after Thomas Bewick's pioneering technical advances in wood engraving that it became common to acknowledge the artistic and technical expertise of book and magazine illustrators. Although widely regarded as the patriarch of the *Golden Age*, Walter Crane (1845-1915) started his career as an anonymous illustrator – gradually building his reputation through striking designs, famous for their sharp outlines and flat tints of colour. Like many other great illustrators to follow, Crane operated within many different mediums; a lifelong disciple of William Morris and a member of the Arts and Crafts Movement, he designed all manner of objects including wallpaper, furniture, ceramic ware and even whole interiors. This incredibly important and inclusive phase of British design proved to have a lasting impact on illustration both in the United Kingdom and Europe as well as America.

The artists involved in the Arts and Crafts Movement attempted to counter the ever intruding Industrial Revolution (the first wave of which lasted roughly from 1750-1850) by bringing the values of beautiful and inventive craftsmanship back into the sphere of everyday life. It must be noted that around the turn of the century the boundaries between what would today be termed 'fine art' as opposed to 'crafts' and 'design' were far more fluid and in many cases non-operational, and many illustrators had lucrative painterly careers in addition to their design work. The Romanticism of the *Pre Raphaelite Brotherhood* combined with the intricate curvatures of the *Art Nouveaux* movement provided influential strands running through most illustrators work. The latter especially so for the Scottish illustrator Anne Anderson (1874-1930) as well as the Dutch artist Kay Nielson (1886-1957), who was also inspired by the stunning work of Japanese artists such as Hiroshige.

One of the main accomplishments of nineteenth century illustration lay in its ability to reach far wider numbers than the traditional 'high arts'. In 1892 the American critic William A. Coffin praised the new medium for popularising art; 'more has been done through the medium of illustrated literature... to make the masses of people realise that there is such a thing as art and that it is worth caring about'. Commercially, illustrated publications reached their zenith with the burgeoning 'Gift Book' industry which emerged in the first decade of the twentieth century. The first widely distributed gift book was published in 1905. It comprised of Washington Irving's short story *Rip Van Winkle* with the addition of 51 colour plates by a true master of illustration; Arthur Rackham. Rackham created each plate by first painstakingly drawing his subject in a sinuous pencil line before applying an ink layer – then he used layer upon layer of delicate watercolours to build up the romantic yet calmly ethereal results on which his reputation was constructed. Although Rackham is now one of the most recognisable names in illustration, his delicate palette owed no small debt to Kate Greenaway (1846-1901) – one of the first female illustrators whose pioneering and incredibly subtle use of the watercolour medium resulted in her election to the Royal Institute of Painters in Water Colours, in 1889.

The year before Arthur Rackam's illustrations for *Rip Van Winkle* were published, a young and aspiring French artist by the name of Edmund Dulac (1882-1953) came to London and was to create a similarly impressive legacy. His timing could not have been more fortuitous. Several factors converged around the turn of the century which allowed illustrators and publishers alike a far greater freedom of creativity than previously imagined. The origination of the 'colour separation' practice meant that colour images, extremely faithful to the original artwork could be produced on a grand scale. Dulac possessed a rigorously painterly background (more so than his contemporaries) and was hence able to utilise the new technology so as to allow the colour itself to refine and define an object as opposed to the traditional pen and ink line. It has been estimated that in 1876 there was only one 'colour separation' firm in London, but by 1900 this number had rocketed to fifty. This improvement in printing quality also meant a reduction in labour, and coupled with the introduction of new presses and low-cost supplies of paper this meant that publishers could for the first time afford to pay high wages for highly talented artists.

Whilst still in the U.K, no survey of the *Golden Age of Illustration* would be complete without a mention of the Heath-Robinson brothers. Charles Robinson was renowned for his beautifully detached style, whether in pen and ink or sumptuous watercolours. William (the youngest) was to later garner immense fame for his carefully constructed yet tortuous machines operated by comical, intensely serious attendants. After World War One, the Robinson brothers numbered among the few artists of the Golden Age who continued to regularly produce illustrated works. But as we move towards the United States, one illustrator - Howard Pyle (1853-1911) stood head and shoulders above his contemporaries as the most distinguished illustrator of the age. From 1880 onwards Pyle illustrated over 100 volumes, yet it was not quantity which ensured his precedence over other American (and European) illustrators, but quality.

Pyle's sumptuous illustrations benefitted from a meticulous composition process livened with rich colour and deep recesses, providing a visual framework in which tales such as *Robin Hood* and *The Four Volumes of the Arthurian Cycle* could come to life. These are publications which remain continuous good sellers up till the present day. His flair and originality combined with a thoroughness of planning and execution were principles which he passed onto his many pupils at the *Drexel Institute of Arts and Sciences*. Two such pupils were Jessie Willcox Smith (1863-1935) who went on to illustrate books such as *The Water Babies* and *At the Back of North Wind* and perhaps most famously Maxfield Parrish (1870-1966) who became famed for luxurious colour (most remarkably demonstrated in his blue paintings) and imaginative designs; practices in no short measure gleaned from his tutor. As an indication of Parrish's popularity, in 1925 it was estimated that one fifth of American households possessed a Parrish reproduction.

As is evident from this brief introduction to the 'Golden Age of Illustration', it was a period of massive technological change and artistic ingenuity. The legacy of this enormously important epoch lives on in the present day – in the continuing popularity and respect afforded to illustrators, graphic and fine artists alike. This *Origins of Fairy Tales from around the World* series will hopefully provide a fascinating insight into an era of intense historical and creative development, bringing both little known stories, and the art that has accompanied them, back to life.

Other titles in the 'Origins of
Fairy Tales from Around the World' series...